W9-AXF-241

TWELVE BELLS FOR SANTA

An I CAN READ Book®

Weekly Reader Books presents

TWELVE BELLS FOR SANTA

by Crosby Bonsall

HARPER & ROW, PUBLISHERS
New York, Hagerstown, San Francisco, London

This book is a presentation of Weekly Reader Books. Weekly Reader Books offers book clubs for children from preschool through junior high school.

For further information write to:
Weekly Reader Books
1250 Fairwood Ave.
Columbus, Ohio 43216

 Printed in the United States of America. For information address Harper & Row, Publishers, Inc., 10 East 53rd Street, New York, N.Y. 10022. Published simultaneously in Canada by Fitzhenry & Whiteside Limited, Toronto.

Library of Congress Cataloging in Publication Data
Bonsall, Crosby
Twelve bells for Santa.

(An I can read book)
SUMMARY: Three Children, off to the North Pole to deliver twelve chocolate bells to Santa for winning a contest, become very hungry on the way.
[1. Santa Claus–Fiction. 2. Christmas stories] I. Title.
PZ7.B64265Tw [E] 76-58714
ISBN 0-06-020581-4
ISBN 0-06-020582-2 lib. bdg.

MERRY
CHRISTMAS
RITA

CHRISTMAS IS COMING

CHAPTER ONE

Everyone came to the Christmas party
dressed as Santa Claus.
There was a prize
for the best Santa Claus.

Some of the Santas had reindeer,

and some of the Santas did not.

There was no prize

for the best reindeer.

There was a Christmas tree.
Everyone was going
to help trim it.

But there was a lot of noise.

Dancer bit Comet.

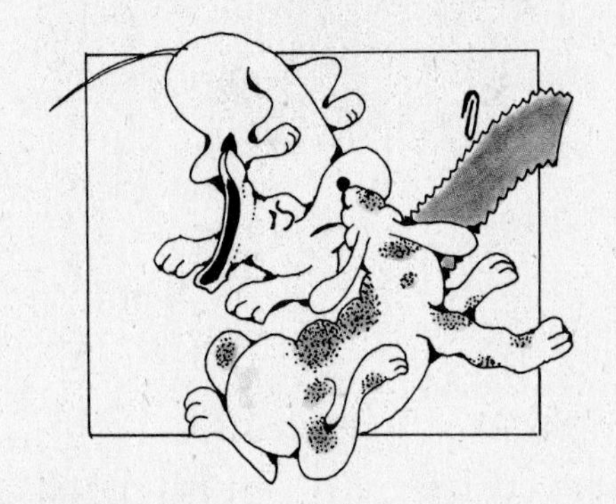

Prancer bit Dancer.

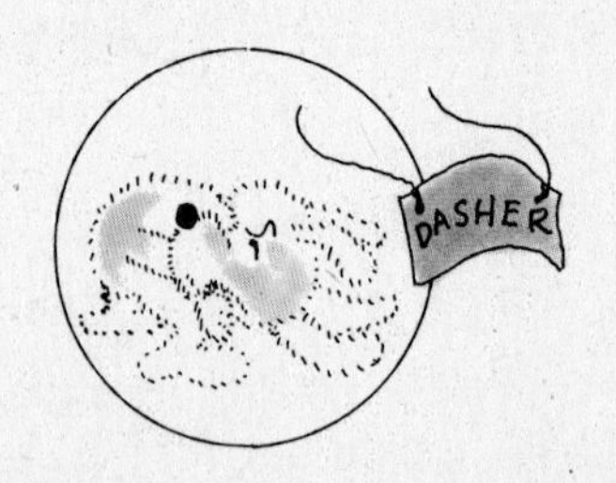

And Dasher bit his own tail.

All the reindeer barked.

All the Santas yelled.

All except one Santa.

He was trimming the tree.

"What a big kid,"

a little Santa said.

"Who is he?"

"I don't know,"

said a girl Santa,

"but he has put presents

under the tree."

"He will get the prize,"

said the other Santas.

"He is the best."

One minute the big Santa
was putting the star on the tree.

The next minute he was gone.

And the reindeer

were dashing out the door.

"Did that Santa
call our reindeer?"
a little Santa asked.

"Where did he go?"
another Santa wondered.
"What are those bells?"
They ran outside.

Their reindeer

sat in the snow.

And they were alone.

But in the snow

were the tracks

of a sleigh.

And in the air
was the sound
of sleigh bells.

"Oh!" cried the
littlest Santa,
"Look!"

Around the neck

of each of their reindeer

hung a star just like the one

Santa had put on the tree.

"No wonder he was the best,"

a Santa said.

"He was the real one."

And they all shouted,

"MERRY CHRISTMAS, SANTA CLAUS!

You win the prize!"

"I will pick it up next year,"

called a voice from high in the sky.

"AND MERRY CHRISTMAS TO ALL OF YOU

CHAPTER TWO

The party was over,

and everyone was happy.

Everyone except Bee

and Wilma and Norman.

They were not happy.

Bee was holding Santa's prize.
It was a box full of
twelve chocolate bells.

"Santa can't wait a whole year
for his prize," Bee said.
"It isn't fair," Wilma cried.

“I do not want to wait
a whole year for MY presents,”
Norman told them.
“Santa will bring MY presents
on Christmas Eve, won’t he?”

Norman said,
"I asked Santa for a sled,
a radio, a singing doll,
a whole chicken dinner
all to myself,
a space suit,
a set of drums, a tree house,
a watch, a book on lions,
a cowboy hat, a can of worms,
a pair of tap shoes."
Norman was out of breath.
"Of all the piggy things,"
Wilma said.

Bee said, "You are not
a nice person, Norman."
Wilma hit him with a snowball.

"And twelve ice-cream cones,"
Norman said
with a mouth full of snow.

Bee said, “If you want Santa
to bring your presents,
you better bring Santa his prize.”
“I don’t know anybody
going to the North Pole,”
Norman said.
“We could mail it,” Wilma said.

"It might not get there," Bee said.

"We could make sure

if we took it ourselves."

"All the way to the North Pole?"

Wilma shouted.

"Sure," Bee said.

“How will we find the North Pole?”

Norman asked.

“Easy,” Bee said. “I will make a map.

I will put the North Pole

on top of the map.

The North Pole is always

on top of the map,” Bee told them.

“Tomorrow,” Bee said, “we will meet
here in the school yard
and zip right up to the North Pole.
We can’t miss.”
“Yes, we can,” said Norman.

CHAPTER THREE

The next morning

Bee met Norman and Wilma.

Bee showed them her map.

"I do not like that map," Norman said.

"My house is as big as yours."

Wilma said, "What's that blob

on the bottom?"

Bee said, "It's a mistake."

"Some mistake!" Wilma said.

"The North Pole is not far from school," Wilma said. "I told you it was not far," Bee said. "If we hurry, we can be back by lunch."

They walked up the hill.

Bee was holding the map

with the North Pole on top.

Wilma was watching Norman.

Norman was carrying the prize.

After a while Norman called out,
"Is it the North Pole soon?
I am hungry."

"In a little while," Bee said.
"But I am hungry NOW," Norman said.
"Well, there is nothing to eat NOW,"
Bee told him.

"Except the twelve chocolate bells,"

Wilma said.

"If we each eat one chocolate bell,

Santa will not mind,"

Norman said.

"Then, when Santa invites us

to have a bell,

we can say no thank you,"

Wilma said.

"I will say yes," Norman said.

"You are not a nice person,"

Wilma told him.

"No," said Bee,

"you are not a nice person."

"I am hungry, too," Bee said.

"Maybe if we each

eat just one bell

Santa will not mind."

"Santa will like that," Norman said.

They each ate a chocolate bell.

Then Bee picked up the map and they walked on.
Norman was carrying the box of nine chocolate bells.

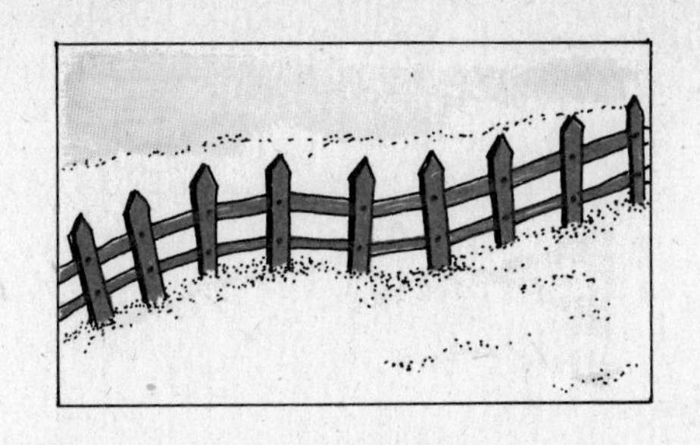

n their way

ey saw

picket fence

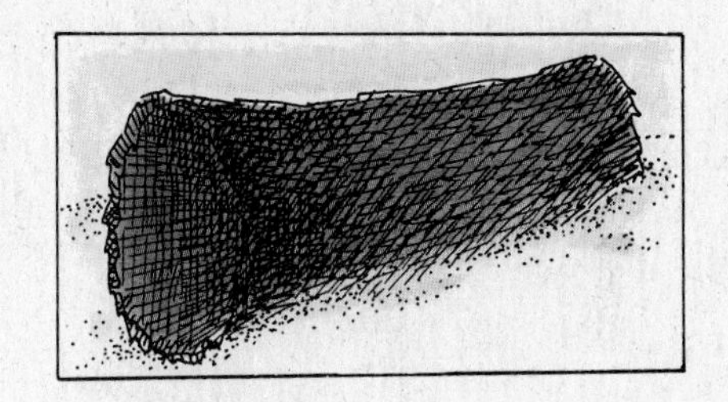

nd a hollow log.

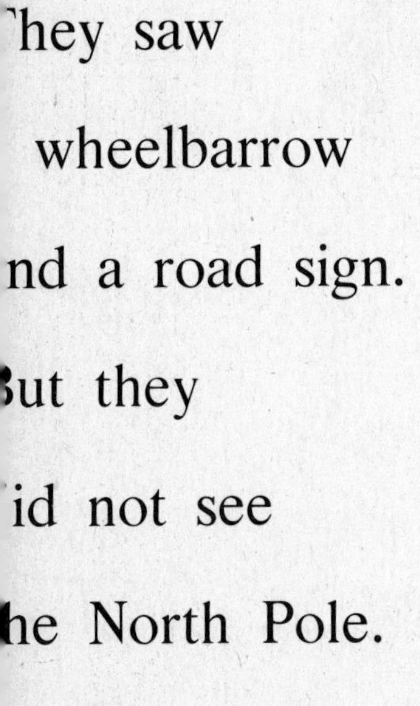

hey saw

wheelbarrow

nd a road sign.

ut they

id not see

he North Pole.

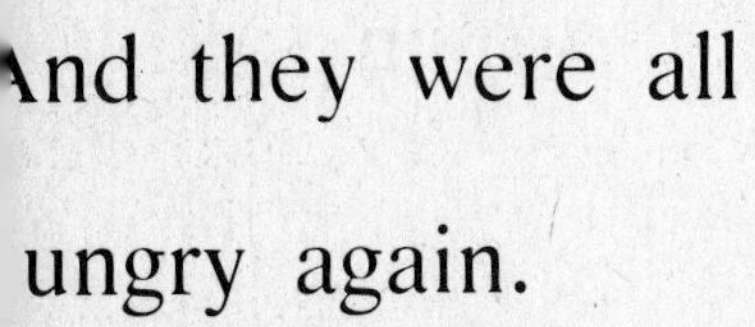

nd they were all

ungry again.

"If we each eat
one chocolate bell
we will have six left
for Santa Claus," Norman said.
And Wilma said,
"That's a whole half dozen!"

"Half a dozen chocolate bells
is a nice prize," Bee said.
"Santa will not mind.
Santa will like that," Norman said.
They each ate a chocolate bell.

Bee picked up the map
and they walked on.
Norman was carrying the box
of six chocolate bells.

“Hey,” Norman cried, “I am hungry again. Could I have just one chocolate bell?”

"If he has one, I want one,"
Wilma shouted.
"If we each have one," Bee said,
"that will leave
only three for Santa Claus."

"Then we can each
give him one," Wilma said.
"Santa will like that," Norman sai
They each ate a chocolate bell.

Bee picked up the map

and they walked on.

Norman was carrying the box

of three chocolate bells.

It started to snow.

The North Pole seemed

very far away.

"I am tired," Wilma grumbled.

"This box is heavy,"

Norman complained.

"Be quiet," Bee said.

"I see the North Pole

just where I said it was."

"Where?" Norman yelled.

"Is it that thing

over there?" Wilma shouted.

"Sure it is," Bee said. "RUN!"

They ran.

And they ran.

And they fell down.

And then they got up.

And then they ran some more.

"There's a sidewalk,"

Bee shouted.

"And a fence and a gate,"

Wilma cried.

"Is it the North Pole yet?"

Norman yelled.

"It is the North Pole," Bee said.

"WE ARE BACK

WHERE WE STARTED,"

Wilma hollered.

"You didn't keep

the North Pole on the top!"

Wilma shouted.

Norman began to yell.

"You said the North Pole

was ALWAYS on the top!

I HATE YOU!

I WANT SANTA CLAUS!"

And Norman began to cry.

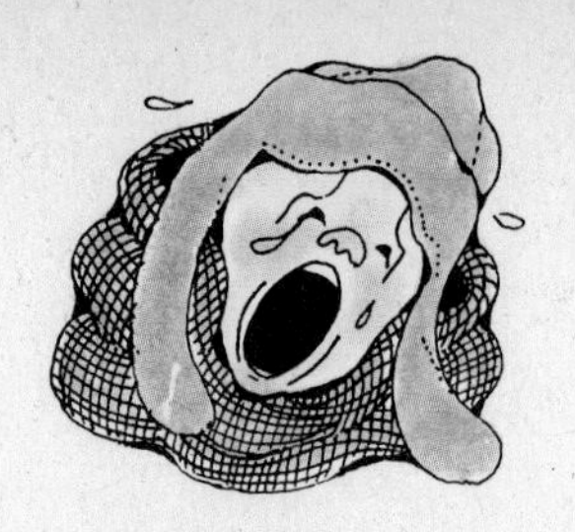  

"Please, Norman, don't cry," Bee said

"Blow your nose, Norman," Wilma sai

"Norman, use my hanky," Bee said.

"He is red as a beet," Wilma said.

"Eat a chocolate bell," Bee said.

"Have another," Wilma said.

"Here, take the last one," Bee said.

Norman stopped crying.

Norman ate three chocolate bells.

He ate them all at once.

"Santa will not mind," Norman said.

"Yes he will," Bee said.

"We ate his prize."

Norman said, "We will get

another prize next year.

And we already have a neat box

to put it in.

Santa will like that."

"I hope so," Wilma said.

"I guess so," said Bee.

Norman began to cry again.

"What's the matter NOW?"

Bee shouted.

"I want to see Santa Claus,"
Norman howled.

"You will see him tonight," Bee cried.
"Tonight is Christmas Eve!"
Norman went home right away.

“Well,” Bee began.

But Wilma was gone.

Bee picked up the empty box.
Then she threw her map in
the trash basket
and walked slowly home.

Bee did not see Santa Claus

that frosty Christmas Eve.

But Santa saw Bee.

Santa did not need a map.

Wilma did not see Santa Claus

that starry Christmas Eve.

Wilma was dreaming

of chocolate bells.

Santa did not mind that.

Norman did not see Santa Claus
that snowy Christmas Eve.
Norman was sleeping.
Norman was not crying.
Santa liked that.

Santa is a nice person.

Merry Christmas, Santa Claus.

Merry Christmas, everyone.